COWGIRL

Grit

BY JAKE MADDOX

text by Cari Meister
illustrated by Katie Wood

STONE ARCH BOOKS
a capstone imprint

Jake Maddox Girl Sports Stories are published by Stone Arch Books
a Capstone imprint
1710 Roe Crest Drive
North Mankato, Minnesota 56003
www.mycapstone.com

Text and illustrations © 2018 Stone Arch Books

Library of Congress Cataloging-in-Publication data is available
on the Library of Congress website.

ISBN: 978-1-4965-5847-3 (library binding) — 978-1-4965-5849-7 (paperback)
— 978-1-4965-5851-0 (ebook PDF)

Summary: Sydney feels out of place at her grandfather's ranch. So she's
practicing pole bending in secret rather than risk embarrassing herself
in front of the more experienced cowboys and cowgirls. Will Sydney be
able to face her fears, saddle up, and compete in the upcoming rodeo?

Designer: Brent Slingsby

Production Specialist: Tori Abraham

Design Elements: Shutterstock: kiyanochka1

Printed and bound in Canada.
010805S18

TABLE OF CONTENTS

CHAPTER ONE

Change of Plans

Sydney Todachine jumped off the last bus step. "Fifth grade is over!" she said.

"Next year we'll be in middle school!" shouted her best friend, McKenna.

"But first," Syd said, "there'll be a whole summer of hanging out at the beach."

"And the mall," McKenna added.

"It'll be perfect," said Syd as she opened the door to her house. But then she stopped. "Mom! What are you doing home?"

Syd's parents were zoologists at the San Diego Zoo. They were never home before six. Yet there her mom was.

Dr. Todachine squealed. "You'll never believe it!" she said. "Remember that research trip your dad and I applied for? It was to study anteaters in the Amazon."

Syd nodded slowly. "Yeah, the one you didn't get?"

"Well, two of the researchers they had picked can't make it," Dr. Todachine explained. "So now we're going!"

"That's so cool!" McKenna exclaimed.

Syd gave her mom a hug. "Congrats, Mom," she said. "When do you go?"

Dr. Todachine stopped smiling. "That's the thing, Syd. We have to leave tomorrow."

"Tomorrow?" Syd repeated. She let go of her mom.

"I'm sorry it's so sudden. But it's a great opportunity," said Dr. Todachine. "Dad is at the zoo finishing up a few things. I'm here to start packing."

"How long will you be gone?" asked Syd.

"All summer," Dr. Todachine replied.

McKenna jumped in. "That's perfect!" she said. "Syd can stay with me!"

"That's nice of you, McKenna, but Syd's dad and I have already made plans," Dr. Todachine said. She turned toward Syd. "You'll be spending the summer with your grandpa."

"What?" Syd asked, shocked. "I have to stay on the rez for the whole summer?"

Syd's grandpa owned a ranch on the Navajo Nation. It was an American Indian reservation that went into Arizona, New Mexico, and Utah.

"You always say you never get to see Grandpa," her mom replied. "You used to beg to stay on the ranch."

"Like when I was eight!" huffed Syd. She couldn't talk about this any more. She ran to her room. McKenna followed behind.

Syd flopped onto her bed. "I can't believe my parents are doing this to me!" she said.

"At least your grandpa has horses," McKenna said. "You love horses."

"I do love horses, and I do want to see my grandpa," Syd said. "But you don't get it. I'm a city girl. I haven't even visited the ranch since I was eight. How will I fit in?"

CHAPTER TWO

Culture Shock

It all happened so fast. The next morning, Syd packed, said goodbye to her mom and dad, and then boarded the airplane. Before she knew it, Syd was getting off the plane.

Syd's grandpa, Eddy Todachine, was waiting for her. He immediately wrapped her in a giant hug.

"Sydney! It's been too long," said Grandpa Eddy.

Syd smiled. "I missed you too, Grandpa."

"Ever since you won the mutton-busting championship when you were eight, I've been waiting for you to come back," he continued. "So what rodeo event will you try this summer? Maybe barrel racing?"

Syd stared down at the airport carpet. It was hard to think about rodeo right now. She missed home too much. *Plus, it's been so long since I've been on the ranch,* she thought. *How could I ever be at the same level as the other riders?*

Grandpa Eddy patted her on the back. "Well, there's lots of time to talk about all that," he said.

They loaded her luggage into Grandpa Eddy's truck. Syd stared out the window as they began the drive to the Navajo Nation.

* * *

As her grandpa drove up the dirt road, Syd got a pit in her stomach. The ranch hadn't changed at all. There was the house, the barn, and the corrals. It was nothing like the big city of San Diego.

I wish I didn't have to be here. Staying with McKenna would've been so much better. Syd fought back tears as she got out of the truck.

Grandpa Eddy pointed to the barn. "We have ten horses now. A ranch hand helps me with them. Over there are his kids, the Deckers. Patrick is fourteen, and Jayli is eleven. They can't wait to ride with you."

Sydney watched Patrick and Jayli in the outdoor arena. They were working their horses around three barrels. The riders took turns whipping around them.

Patrick and Jayli look so good, thought Syd. *I can't ride like that! I'll never fit in with them.*

Syd's grandpa interrupted her thoughts. "I don't know if your dad told you, but your cousin Hadley is here too," he added.

Syd groaned. "Why?"

"He just is," Grandpa Eddy replied with a shrug. "Plus, he's family. Try to be nice."

It wasn't Syd who had to be reminded to be nice. Hadley was the mean one. He always made Syd feel dumb about ranch things. Hadley had grown up around rodeos. In fact, he was probably staying here because his mom was busy competing.

"Dinner should be ready," Grandpa Eddy said. "Let's head inside."

They went into the house. Hadley was already sitting at the table. Syd and her grandpa joined him.

"Hi, Hadley," said Syd.

Hadley pushed his long black hair out of his eyes. He looked Syd up and down. Then he laughed under his breath.

This is not going well, Syd thought.

"So," Grandpa Eddy said as he passed Syd a plate of roasted corn. "Your dad says that you've been riding."

"A little," Syd replied. "Mom's friend has a horse. She lets me ride him. He's older, so I mostly walk him on trails or by the beach."

"Wow, that sounds really exciting," Hadley said, rolling his eyes. "I bet you think you're ready to be a rodeo champion."

Sydney felt her cheeks grow warm. "Of course not," she said.

"So you just came here to play cowgirl for a while?" Hadley added. "And then go back to your fancy life in San Diego —"

"That's enough, Hadley," said Grandpa Eddy, cutting in.

Syd put her fork down. "Sorry, I'm really tired. Can I go to bed?" she asked her grandpa.

Grandpa Eddy looked concerned, but he nodded. "Sure. You've had a long day."

"Thanks for dinner," Syd added. Then she escaped to her bedroom.

Syd sat on the bed and took out her cell phone. She wanted to text McKenna. But there was no signal.

Syd sighed and look around the room. It was so different from home. It even smelled different. Everything felt foreign.

I just want to go home, she thought. Syd cried into the pillow and fell asleep.

CHAPTER THREE

Midnight

CRACK! BOOM!

Syd woke to a thunderstorm. Thunder boomed, and lightning lit up the night sky.

She heard something else too. A banging sound was coming from the barn. *Could it be one of the horses?* Syd wondered. *I'll check it out first before bothering Grandpa.*

A minute later, Syd was running through the rain to the barn. She heard the banging again as she went inside. In the back, a horse was whinnying and snorting.

Syd walked over to the horse's stall.
He was a black quarter horse. His eyes
darted back and forth. He was terrified.

"Hey there," Syd said calmly and quietly.
"It's OK. It's just a storm."

The horse stopped kicking and looked at
her. Syd found his nameplate on the stall.

"Hi, Midnight," she said. "I'm Syd.
I'm new to the ranch. It's nice to meet you."

A crack of thunder rattled the doors.
Midnight jumped and squealed again.

"Don't be scared," she said. "Look,
I'm OK, and I'm much smaller than you."

Syd's talking seemed to calm Midnight.
She kept going. "You must feel trapped.
I feel trapped on this ranch. I can't talk to
my friends. Everything is so different. But if
I kick and yell, I won't get to go home."

Every time Syd spoke, Midnight settled. When he was calm enough, Syd opened his stall door and went in. She let him smell her first. His soft black lips nibbled her hair.

Syd laughed. "Hey! Have some manners!"

Syd started rubbing Midnight's neck. She found his favorite spot — just behind his left ear. After getting brushes from the tack room, she brushed him down. Soon Midnight was totally calm.

"You're a beautiful horse. I'd love to ride you," she told him. "Are you a good boy under the saddle?"

Midnight nickered.

"I knew it," said Syd.

But, she thought, *I don't want anyone to see me ride. What if I look like I don't know what I'm doing? Hadley would tease me for sure.*

Soon the rain slowed and the storm ended. It was almost morning. Syd gave Midnight a final pat and stepped out of the stall.

As she closed the stall door, there was a *thunk* in the hayloft. Syd looked up, but she didn't see anything.

It was probably just a barn cat chasing a mouse, she thought.

Syd turned back to Midnight. He gazed at her with his big brown eyes.

"I'll be back," she promised. Then she slipped out of the barn as the sun rose over the ranch.

CHAPTER FOUR

Ranch Cowboys

After Syd had eaten breakfast and had gotten dressed, she rushed back to the barn. She wanted to check on her new friend. But Midnight's stall was empty.

The ranch hand must've let the horses out into the pasture, Syd thought.

On her way to the pasture, Syd spotted Jayli and Patrick. They were riding in the outdoor arena. In the center stood six tall poles in a line.

Jayli galloped past the poles. When she reached the top one, she turned. She quickly wove her horse down and back up the line.

When they stopped, Jayli saw Syd and waved. Syd was nervous about meeting the ranch kids, but she walked over.

"Hi!" Jayli said. "You must be Syd. I'm Jayli. This is Fresca." She patted the big brown horse.

"Fresca is beautiful!" Syd replied.

"Thanks," said Jayli. "Your grandpa lets me ride her in the rodeo. This year I'm doing barrel racing and pole bending."

Patrick trotted over. "Hey, I'm Patrick. Have you ever been to a rodeo?"

"I went the last time I was here," Syd said. "All I remember are fast horses and dust. I don't know much about pole binding."

Patrick chuckled. "It's pole *bending*," he corrected.

"Oh, oops," Syd muttered. She knew she would embarrass herself in front of the other kids.

"It's all right. Pole bending is when a rider makes figure eights through a line of poles. That's what you saw Jayli do," Patrick explained. "In barrel racing, a rider goes around barrels in a cloverleaf pattern. Fastest time wins for both events."

"There's a rodeo tomorrow. You should come!" Jayli added. "You'll see the best barrel racer on the rez. Patrick and his horse, Chance, won the championship last year."

Wow, Jayli and Patrick are real rodeo pros, Syd thought. *I'm not good enough to ride with them!*

"I'll be there. Grandpa lives and breathes rodeo, so I don't have much of a choice," Syd told them. Then she looked around. "Hey, have you guys seen Midnight?"

"He's over in the front pasture," Jayli said, pointing toward a little hill. "Are you going to ride him?"

Syd wasn't sure what to say. She wanted more than anything to ride Midnight. But she didn't want to tell Jayli and Patrick that. Not yet.

I just want to see how it goes first, Syd thought. *Without cowboys and cowgirls watching me!*

Syd shrugged. "Maybe sometime," she told Jayli.

* * *

As soon as Syd entered the pasture, Midnight came trotting over. He nudged her pocket.

"How did you know?" asked Syd as she pulled out a carrot. Midnight crunched happily while Syd rubbed behind his ears.

Syd looked around. No one was watching. She climbed up onto Midnight's back. He didn't seem to mind.

"I really miss my friends and the San Diego beaches. But maybe riding you would be almost as fun," Syd told Midnight. "Do you think we could do the poles like Jayli and Fresca? That seems pretty cool."

Just then something caught Syd's eye. It was Hadley. He was walking along the pasture's fence.

Syd quickly jumped off the horse. She didn't want Hadley to see her on Midnight. He would just accuse her of being a fake cowgirl again.

I wish I had some time riding by myself. Then I won't have to worry about looking silly, Syd thought.

She patted Midnight's neck. "But how can I ride with no one watching?" she whispered.

Midnight stamped his foot. He threw his head up toward the sky.

"That's it!" said Syd. "I'll ride at night when everyone is sleeping. After all, your name *is* Midnight."

CHAPTER FIVE

Night Riding

That night, Syd crawled out of bed at 2 a.m. When she went into the barn, Midnight greeted her with a soft nicker.

"I know it's the middle of the night," she said. "But this will be fun. I promise!"

Syd led Midnight out and brushed him down. She found his saddle and bridle in the tack room. When he was ready, they went to the outdoor arena.

Syd knew it could be dangerous riding at night, so she flicked on lights to brighten up the arena. Luckily, the arena was on the far side of the barn. If anyone looked out from the house, they would not be able to see them.

Syd could ride without worrying about anyone watching.

For the first couple minutes, she got used to being in the saddle. They walked around the arena. Then they did a few circles and bending paths called serpentines.

Syd smiled. Midnight responded to every nudge she made.

She gave him a little squeeze with her legs. He went right into a trot. Without the loud storm, Midnight was willing and calm.

"Good boy," she said.

The night air cooled her face and hands, but Syd didn't care. She felt free riding Midnight.

Maybe being on the ranch isn't so bad after all, she thought.

After working Midnight for about twenty minutes, she let him cool down. "That's enough for our first night," she said, patting his neck.

The two went back into the barn. Syd brushed Midnight and cleaned the tack. Then she quietly snuck back to the house.

CHAPTER SIX

Rodeo Day

The next morning came fast. Syd groaned as she turned off her beeping alarm. She wouldn't be able to sleep in today. It was the first rodeo of the season.

Grandpa Eddy, Hadley, and Syd got to the rodeo grounds just as the sun was rising. None of them were competing, but Syd's grandpa was the announcer. He was always there early.

Grandpa Eddy went to check on the sound system. So Syd walked over to the food trucks to get hot chocolate. Hadley disappeared.

Syd watched trucks and trailers arrive. Riders began unloading their horses. Then Syd saw the Deckers pull in. She waved.

Jayli waved back and signaled for Syd to come over. Jayli and Patrick were dressed in their finest show attire. They both had on fancy Western shirts, dark jeans, and belts with giant buckles.

Patrick tipped his hat. "Mornin'."

"Good morning," said Syd. "You two look ready to go."

"You know it!" said Jayli. "Hey, can you hold Fresca and Chance while we register?"

Syd nodded. She took the horses' reins as Jayli and Patrick went off. The horses swished their tails and waited patiently.

"Whoa, you have two horses?" asked a voice. "You're really playing cowgirl now."

Syd looked behind her. It was Hadley. "The Deckers asked me to hold their horses. What's wrong with that?" she asked.

"It's just funny watching a city girl try to act like a cowgirl," Hadley said. Then he walked off again.

Just as Hadley left, Patrick came back. "I don't get it," Syd told Patrick. "Why is Hadley so rude to me?"

"He'll come around," said Patrick. "He's probably just jealous because your life seems so good. You know, he never met his dad. And his mom . . . She kind of ditched him at the ranch. It must be rough."

Syd was surprised. Her dad didn't talk much about Syd's aunt. Syd had no idea she had left. It didn't give Hadley an excuse to be so mean, but Syd started to look at him in a new way.

Just then, Syd heard her grandpa's voice over the loudspeaker. "Ladies and gentlemen, take your seats! The first rodeo of the season is about to begin. If you're a visitor, welcome to the Navajo Nation."

Syd went into the stands as the rodeo started. Mutton busting was first. Little cowpokes tried to hang on to sheep as they ran around the arena.

Syd laughed, remembering when she won that event four years ago. *The ribbon is still hanging in my room,* she thought with pride.

Pole bending was next. Jayli was the first to go in her age group.

The buzzer sounded. Jayli was off. She slapped the reins on Fresca's neck to get her to gallop fast. Rider and horse carefully and quickly bent around the poles. They finished the run in 22.651 seconds.

"Yeah, Jayli!" Syd cheered.

The next rider wasn't as smooth and knocked over a pole. That added a penalty of five seconds to her time.

Syd smiled as she watched the other riders weave through the poles. *I bet Midnight would be great at this,* she thought.

As the rodeo went on, Syd tried to pay attention to Patrick's barrel race run. But she couldn't focus on the arena. She kept imagining herself on Midnight, competing in the next rodeo.

CHAPTER SEVEN

Pole Bending Practice

The next night, Syd's alarm went off again at 2 a.m. She rubbed her eyes and rolled over. She was so tired! But then she popped up.

Riding! Midnight! Syd thought. She got dressed and headed out to the barn.

She found the poles stacked on the side of the arena. She set them up like they were at the rodeo. Six poles placed twenty-one feet apart.

"We're not going for speed," Syd said as she got on Midnight. "Not yet. First, we'll do the poles at a walk."

Syd walked Midnight straight past the poles. When they reached the top one, she turned him around it. They weaved around each pole. At the end of the line, they turned and weaved in the other direction.

"Nice work, Midnight," she said. "Let's try it at a trot."

Midnight trotted forward. But Syd wasn't watching where she was going. They knocked over a pole. Syd set it back up. After a few tries, they made all of the turns without hitting any poles.

"Not perfect, but not bad," she said to Midnight. "Our turns could be a bit cleaner. But I think we're ready to try it at a canter."

Syd pushed Midnight forward. It was too fast. They missed the second turn.

"Whoa! Easy, boy," Syd said to Midnight, pulling back on the reins.

Syd took a deep breath and tried again. She kicked his side, and he went right into a canter.

It was hard doing everything right at the faster speed. Either they missed bending around a pole, or she took Midnight in too close. They knocked over a few more poles.

But they kept trying. Soon, Midnight turned in exactly the right places, and they weren't hitting the poles. Syd brought Midnight to a walk.

"That was awesome!" she said. "We're getting so much better. If we keep this up, we could actually compete!"

* * *

During the following day, Syd watched Jayli train with Fresca. She wanted more pointers on pole bending. She studied the other girl closely.

The next night, Syd practiced just like the cowgirl. Midnight was responding well. He cantered through the pattern without any problems. Syd was feeling more confident.

"I think we're almost ready to practice during the day," she said, patting Midnight. "Let's do it one more time."

But before she made her first bend, something crashed outside of the arena. It startled Midnight. He kicked out.

Syd fell to the ground and landed on her arm. "Ugh!" she cried.

Dazed, Syd stood up. She touched her arm and winced. It was sore, but not broken. Midnight stood still, panting.

Syd walked over to him. "Don't worry. It's not your fault. Something spooked you," she said. Tears sprang to her eyes. "But maybe Hadley was right. I'm no cowgirl. I'm just trying to act like one."

Defeated, Syd grabbed Midnight's reins and led him back to the barn.

CHAPTER EIGHT

Secret's Out

The next morning, Syd sat down for breakfast with her grandpa and Hadley. She rubbed her arm. A bruise had appeared during the night.

"Are you OK?" Grandpa Eddy asked.

Syd tried to hide her arm under the table. "Yeah," she replied.

"Actually, she fell off Midnight last night," Hadley said. "But it wasn't a bad fall."

Syd stared at her cousin in disbelief. How did he know? *There were strange noises in the barn and by the arena,* she thought. *Those noises must have been him!*

"She's been pole bending at night," Hadley continued. "Training, I guess."

Grandpa Eddy smiled. "That's great!" he said. "Don't see why you're riding at night, though. How do you like Midnight?"

But Syd didn't reply. She just stared at her cousin. "You were spying on me? Why can't you just leave me alone?"

Hadley looked surprised, and a little hurt. "I was making sure you were OK. It's dangerous to ride at night, you know."

"Yeah, whatever," Syd huffed. "You were waiting until I messed up. Then you could point out what a bad rider I am."

"Well," Hadley said, "maybe that was my plan at the beginning, but . . ."

"But what?" Grandpa Eddy asked.

"It changed," Hadley mumbled. He glanced at Syd. "Look, you're a pretty good rider. You and Midnight are a great fit."

"So why didn't you just let me know you were there?" Syd asked.

"You would have stopped riding if you knew I was watching," Hadley argued. He paused. "Midnight was my mom's horse. It's just nice that he's being ridden again."

Then Hadley stood up. Syd watched as he went outside. She didn't know Midnight had been his mom's horse.

"Aren't you going to talk to Hadley?" Syd asked her grandpa. "He seemed upset."

Grandpa Eddy shook his head. "I know when Hadley wants to be left alone. This is one of those times." Then he asked, "So, are you getting ready for the rodeo?"

Syd shrugged. "I'm not sure I'm cut out for it. I'll probably just embarrass myself."

"Well, did you like pole bending?" her grandpa asked. "Were you having fun?"

"Yeah, it's been really fun," Syd admitted. Plus, riding made her feel at home.

"Then why worry about what other people think?" Grandpa Eddy asked.

Syd thought for a moment. "You're right," she said finally. "Riding makes me happy. So I'm not going to let anything stop me!"

Grandpa Eddy grinned. "That's the spirit! I know Sydney Todachine can do anything she puts her mind to."

CHAPTER NINE

Back in the Saddle

After breakfast, Syd went looking for Jayli and Patrick. They were in the arena practicing for the next rodeo. Syd wasn't going to keep her pole bending a secret anymore. She told them about her night riding and her fall.

"I'm so excited you're pole bending!" Jayli exclaimed. "It'll be fun practicing together."

"And don't worry about the fall," Patrick added. "It happens to everyone. You just need to get back on."

Syd grinned. It seemed silly that she thought the Deckers would tease her about riding. They were so encouraging.

"I can help practice too," a voice said.

The trio turned. They hadn't seen Hadley walk up.

"If you want," Hadley added. He looked at their surprised faces. "What? It's not like I can't ride."

"That's true," Jayli agreed. "You used to be a better barrel racer than Patrick."

"Hey!" Patrick said, crossing his arms.

Jayli laughed. "It's the truth!"

"Really? Why did you stop?" Syd asked.

Hadley kicked the dirt. "When my mom left, I didn't feel like doing it anymore. But I think I'd like to start again."

* * *

All day long, Patrick, Jayli, and Hadley worked with Syd on pole bending. Syd made some mistakes, but she didn't feel embarrassed. She was too busy working hard and having fun.

The three other riders gave Syd lots of advice. Their words echoed in her head. *Prepare earlier for the turn. Look ahead to the next pole. Use your outside leg more to guide Midnight.* Syd practiced until she could hardly move.

When they were finishing up, Hadley walked over to Syd. "Hey, you don't look so San Diego anymore," he said, smiling.

Syd smiled too. "No? How do I look?" she asked.

"Like a real cowgirl!" Hadley exclaimed.

"Tomorrow is the rodeo," Jayli pointed out. "You should sign up, Syd. You're totally ready for it."

Syd had been thinking about it all day. *What's the worst that could happen? I could fall off. I could get a slow time. But hey, that's part of it, isn't it?*

Syd looked over at Hadley. "I will if Hadley does."

Hadley groaned, but Syd saw that he was trying to hide a smile. "I guess I don't have a choice," he said. "Grandpa would never forgive me if I had anything to do with you not getting in the ring!"

* * *

As Syd was getting ready for bed that night, the house phone rang. It was her mom. Syd's parents were back in San Diego.

"The mudslides were so bad they sent us home," Dr. Todachine explained. "We'll have to wait until next year for the study."

"I'm sorry, Mom," Syd said. "I know how excited you both were."

"But there's good news too," Dr. Todachine added. "Now that we're back, you can come home whenever you want!"

Syd was stunned. When she first came to the ranch, all she wanted was to go home. But now . . .

"Syd? Are you still there?" her mom asked.

"Yes, I'm here," Syd finally replied. "You know what, Mom? I'm not ready to come home yet."

CHAPTER TEN

Rodeo Rider

The next morning, Hadley and Grandpa Eddy had on their rodeo attire. Each wore cowboy boots, jeans, big belt buckles, and Western shirts. Syd was dressed in jeans and a white button-up shirt.

Hadley tried not to laugh when he saw her. "Is that what you're wearing?" he asked.

Syd looked down and frowned. "I don't have any Western stuff," she said. "Will they disqualify me?"

"No," her grandpa said with a twinkle in his eye. "But I bet I can find something."

Grandpa Eddy disappeared for a few minutes. He came back carrying a big shopping bag. He handed it to Syd.

Syd pulled out a sky blue cowboy hat, a matching plaid shirt, and cowgirl boots. Her mouth dropped open.

"When I found out you were riding, I thought I'd better get you some new rodeo clothes, just in case," Grandpa Eddy explained. "Well, go see if it fits!"

Syd ran to her room and tried everything on. It was different than what she normally wore. She put on the cowboy hat and looked in the mirror. She looked like a true Navajo cowgirl. Then she smiled. It felt good. It felt right.

* * *

Sydney was feeling excited as they unloaded at the rodeo grounds. She brushed Midnight's long mane.

"Just like practice," she whispered to him. "I know you've done this before. Take care of me, OK?"

Midnight nibbled at her hair as her grandpa's voice came over the loudspeaker.

"Welcome to the second rodeo of the season! I'm your announcer, Eddy Todachine. Let's get started with mutton busting."

The first events of the day rushed by. Soon, pole bending was about to begin. Syd hopped onto Midnight.

Grandpa Eddy's voice boomed in the arena. "Now our young cowgirls will compete in pole bending. Miss Jayli Decker is first."

Syd watched from the waiting area. Jayli raced through the poles. She got her best time ever — 22.086 seconds! She was all smiles when she trotted back.

"Nice job!" Syd exclaimed.

"Thanks! Now it's your turn," Jayli added. "You'll do great."

Syd gripped the reins. She was ready.

"Next up, Sydney Todachine riding Midnight!" Grandpa Eddy announced.

Syd kicked Midnight forward. He took off instantly. He seemed to like the energy of the rodeo. He raced down the arena and past the poles.

Syd dropped one hand to the saddle horn. She gripped it as they turned around the top pole. Then they started weaving down the line.

It felt amazing. They floated through the figure eights. Syd kept her focus and guided Midnight. She felt like they were totally in sync.

They weaved back up through the poles. When they had finished, Syd turned Midnight around. They started the straight run back to the finish line.

Syd pushed Midnight as fast as he could go. The crowed whooped and cheered.

"23.981 seconds!" yelled Grandpa Eddy. "Well done! That's my granddaughter, ladies and gentleman. Sydney Todachine!"

Syd was out of breath as she and Midnight trotted back into the waiting area. She couldn't believe it. She had competed!

Jayli came over. "Wow, Syd!" she said. "That was a great run."

"Thanks!" Syd replied. She patted Midnight's neck. "Midnight was wonderful. And with more practice, I think we can do even better at our next rodeo!"

"Absolutely!" said Jayli. "Isn't pole bending the greatest?"

Syd smiled. "I love it. "

Jayli and Syd tied up their horses and gave them some hay. They made it back to the stands in time to watch barrel racing.

Both Patrick and Hadley had great runs. Syd cheered as they quickly turned their horses around the barrels.

Hadley won the event by 0.422 seconds. Patrick came in second.

As the sun set, the Todachines and Deckers began packing. They loaded the trailers and got ready to go home.

Hadley walked over to Syd. "Hey, I wanted to say thank you," he said.

"For what?" Syd asked.

"For getting me riding again," Hadley replied. "I'm sorry I wasn't nice to you when you first came. I didn't know how to act around a city girl."

Syd wasn't sure what to say. So she gave Hadley a hug.

"No problem," she said. Together, they started walking toward their grandpa's truck. "You can make up for it by teaching me how to barrel race . . . since I will be staying all summer!"

Author Bio

Cari Meister has written more than 200 books for children. She lives in Colorado with her husband, four sons, a dog named Koki, and an Arabian horse named Sir William. She loves to visit schools and libraries. Find out more at *carimeister.com*.

Illustrator Bio

Katie Wood fell in love with drawing when she was very small. Since graduating from Loughborough University School of Art and Design in 2004, she has been living her dream working as a freelance illustrator. From her studio in Leicester, England, she creates bright and lively illustrations for books and magazines all over the world.

Glossary

canter (KAN-tuhr)—for a horse to run fairly fast; slower than a gallop

embarrass (em-BAR-uhss)—to cause someone to feel foolish in front of others

gallop (GAL-uhp)—for a horse to run fast

pasture (PASS-chur)—land where farm animals eat grass and exercise

reins (RAYNZ)—straps that control a horse

reservation (rez-er-VAY-shuhn)—a large area of land set aside for American Indians; sometimes called a *rez*

saddle (SAD-uhl)—a seat for a rider that goes on a horse

tack (TAK)—equipment used to control the movement of horses

trot (TROT)—for a horse to move at a quick pace; slower than a canter

Discussion Questions

1. Have you ever felt embarrassed to do something in front of others? How did you overcome your fears? Talk about your experience.

2. Syd could've gone home, but she decided to stay at the ranch for the summer. Were you surprised by Syd's decision? Why or why not? Use examples from the story to support your answer.

3. Discuss how Hadley felt about Syd coming to the ranch. What in the text makes you think that?

Writing Prompts

1. In your own words, write a paragraph summarizing why Syd didn't want to ride Midnight during the day.

2. Write two paragraphs comparing how Syd felt about Hadley at the start of the story and at the end. Be sure to explain what caused the changes. Use examples from the story to support your answer.

3. Pretend you're McKenna. You've found out Syd is feeling out of place and homesick at the ranch. Write a letter to Syd. What advice would you give her?

Rodeo Events

A rodeo is made up of many different events. Riders can compete in several events, but they don't compete in all of them. Which one is your favorite?

BARREL RACING

A rider and horse run a cloverleaf pattern around three barrels. Fastest time wins.

BRONC RIDING

A rider must stay on a wild horse (called a *bronc* or *bronco*) for eight seconds as it bucks. The run is judged and awarded a score out of one hundred points.

BULL RIDING

Participants must ride a bucking bull for eight seconds. Riders receive a score out of fifty points.

GOAT TYING

A rider on horseback races up to a goat that's been tied to a rope. The rider jumps off the horse, grabs the goat, and ties three of its legs together. Fastest time wins.

MUTTON BUSTING

A kids-only event! Young children try to stay on a sheep as it runs around the arena. The rider who stays on the longest wins.

POLE BENDING

A horse and rider weave through a line of six poles. Knocking a pole down adds a five-second penalty. Fastest time wins.

STEER WRESTLING

A rider on horseback chases a steer. The rider jumps off the horse and then wrestles the steer to the ground by grabbing its horns. Fastest time wins.

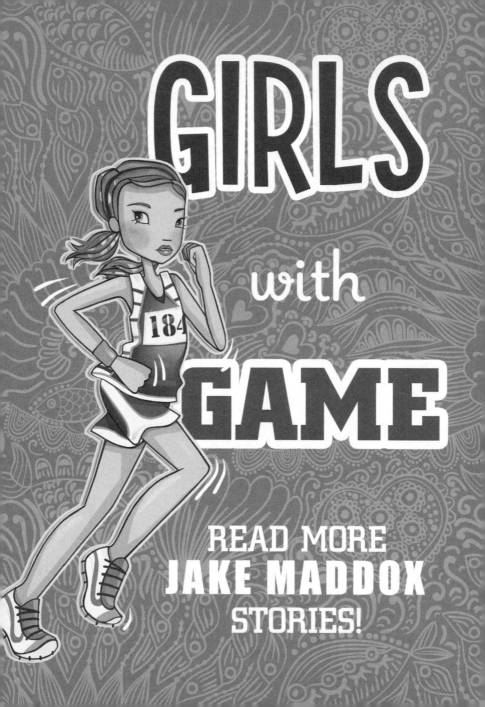

GIRLS

with

GAME

READ MORE
JAKE MADDOX
STORIES!